John Stricker Bradford

Autumn winds

and other poems

John Stricker Bradford

Autumn winds
and other poems

ISBN/EAN: 9783337374693

Printed in Europe, USA, Canada, Australia, Japan

Cover: Foto ©Andreas Hilbeck / pixelio.de

More available books at **www.hansebooks.com**

AUTUMN WINDS,

AND

Other Poems,

BY

J. STRICKER BRADFORD.

———

NEW YORK:

ROBERT M. MALCOLM,

1877.

THIS LITTLE VOLUME

IS RESPECTFULLY DEDICATED

BY

THE AUTHOR,

TO

HIS FRIENDS OF EARLY DAYS.

PREFACE.

The author submits this little volume to the public as a reprint of a volume, bearing the same title, printed in December 1868, but suppressed before many copies had been circulated.

The matter then printed has been carefully revised for this volume which contains several additional poems.

Although a period of eight years has elapsed since the date of this first publication, the preface of the original volume, being as applicable now as then in explantion of the sentiments of the author, is submitted entire—as follows :

"In offering these casual effusions to the public, the author would beg leave to call attention to those having a political tendency, with the explanation that, being a native of a Southern State and a resident in the South at the opening of the Rebellion, and having foreseen its approach, his sentiments, while strongly in sympathy with his Section, were, until the actual outbreak, even more strongly in favor of the peaceful maintenance of the Union, as exemplified on pages 20, 21 and 22, the dates of which are appended. But subsequently, having joined the Southern current, his later sentiments are clearly portrayed in the lines on later pages.

PREFACE.

" Most of these political poems were published at or about their dates, in the local papers of his residence.

" Deeming that now, when the bitterness engendered by the war is passing away. it becomes the duty of every citizen of a common country to cast his drop of oil on the waters, he hopes that neither sectional feeling or party prejudice will too severely criticise the tone or merit of sincere expressions of sentiment."

J. S. B.

WASHINGTON, D. C., Dec. 1, 1876.

CONTENTS.

CONTENTS.

Autumn Winds

And Other Poems.

AUTUMN WINDS.

What have the Autumn winds to tell
 To the red leafed trees as they sweep along
And vibrate to the rising swell
 Their music makes in mournful song?

They sing the dirge of youthful days,
 Whose tints were bright as the leaves they
  bear:
The saddened heart responsive prays,
 For another taste of the joys that were.

They tell the tale of promise broke,
　　Of Spring-time gone, of Summer fled
And echo with the words we spoke
　　In whispers 'ere our Spring was dead.

They sing the dirge of withered leaves,
　　Of blighted faith, of broken trust;
They sing of mis-spent years, whose sheaves
　　Were garnered not, but left to rust.

A TEXT.

"As ye would that men should do to you, do ye also to them likewise."
— LUKE, c. 6; v. 31.

A Christian maxim that but few men keep;
　A noble motto that should guide the good;
The seed from which we richest harvest reap;
　A simple text we all have understood.

Were but these words inscribed on every heart
　To curb the hasty actions of our lives;
How few would suffer from the wounds and smart
　Of conscience, which some selfish deed survives.

How sweetly peaceful would each death-bed be,
　When in the vivid retrospect of years,
The wearied souls looks forth upon the sea
　That breaks beyond this mortal vale of tears.

NAMELESS.

Who hath not felt a mystic dread
  A nameless terror creep,
Across his soul, as memory fled
Back to the uncertain depths and spread
  A pall, vague dark and deep;
Portentous as of threatening ill,
To dimly, indistinctly fill
  And in strange bondage keep
The pulses of the heart, as though
Some pre-existent act would throw
  A shadow o'er his path?
A simple word may forge the chain
But mental effort is all vain
  To break the hold it hath:
With vague pre-science over-wrought
And formless apprehension fought:
  Is this the shade of wrath?

Or of impending woe the shade
By Premonition's force displayed?
  Or some abnormal state
Of mind, or overworking brain,
That poiseless from exciting strain,
  Life's fantasies dilate?
Or from dark Chaos when the Past
Its terrors leave, or omen's cast
  By stern relentless fate?

Mysterious monitor you come
With odors of the silent tomb
  In ghost-like warning grim :
The human mind must bow to thee,
Thou super-human mystery—
  Thou shadow, pale and dim !

OLD VIRGINIA LAND. [1]

Can'st thou, in lonely hours of night,
  When absent from my arm and love,
Forget the sunshine, pure and bright,
  That warmed the hill-side and the grove —
    In Old Virginia Land ?

Can'st thou forget how fondly then,
  We oft-times wander'd side by side,
And plucked the wild flowers in the glen,
  Or watched the rippling brooklet's tide —
    In Old Virginia Land ?

Can'st thou forget the evening shade
  On the vine-wreath'd porch at home ;
Or the moss-grown turf of the silent glade,
  Where the Beech-spring waters foam —
    In Old Virginia Land ?

And can'st thou, not while far away
　　Where northern winds and skies are cold,
Sometimes permit thy thought to stray
　　In memory to the times of old —
　　　　In Old Virginia Land?

ACROSTICS.

I.

Grant that thy wisdom's mantle yet may fall,
　　Encircling some brave soul with saving might:
Or that, responsive to a Nation's call,
　　Reason may dawn dispersing faction's night:
Grant that the Future in our land may be
Enduring Union, Peace and Liberty!

Would thou wer't here, Sage, Hero of thy Time,
　　Among dissensions and 'midst treasons rife;
Secession standing on the verge of crime,
　　Her nervous sons too eager for the strife:
In the dark train Dis-Union comes —
　　North against South, in armed, fierce array;
Grant from our altars, and our homes,
　　This gathering storm may pass away.
Oh save thy country, if thy spirit can,
Nor leave its memory to the sneers of man.

BALTIMORE, DEC. 25, 1860.

II.

Triumphant flag, whose prestige gave
Heaven-born hopes to good and brave,
Exultantly thy glories wave.

Secession's hand thy folds would stain,
Treason and strife breed civil war
Anarchy and crimes profane.
Respect the compact, and maintain,
Sacred, every Stripe and Star.

Are we no longer Union's band,
No longer in her ranks to stand?
Discord's arm would wield the brand!

Saving Banner, still thou'lt shine,
To lead thy sons through battle fires;
Remembrance of the souls divine
In Hero-days, thy name inspires;
Potent to us as to our sires.
Eternal, bright, on History's page,
Shall gleam thy stars, from age to age.

BALTIMORE, March 10, 1861.

HYMN

FOR THE NATION.

God of Mercy, guard and love us;
God of Justice, watch above us,
   In Faction's bondage strong:
'Midst the dangers that surround us
Mend the band that firmly bound us,
   And bound us for so long.

Not as bands of iron bind us,
As, perforce, they had confined us;
   But as with silken chain,
Light of weight and fair to see,
Firm of hold, but seeming free;
   Oh, make it strong again.

Not with blood, to blur and stain it,
Not by War, can we maintain it;
   But Thy all helping hand
Yet may save, where mortals falter;
Should we bend us at Thy altar
   Will Thou not mend the band?

Save us, Thou—who first did guide them,
Save us, Thou—who stood beside them,
   Those heroes brave and free;
Let bands fraternal still unite us,
And Peace, with blessings, still delight us,
   While still we bow to Thee.

March 20th, 1861.

MARYLAND BATTLE SONG. (2)

Hark, to clang and crash of marching squadrons in
  the street,
Hark to the martial music and the measured tramp
  of feet;
Old Maryland is roused and her sons in fierce
  array,
In battle-harness bristling, stand eager for the fray.

For hearth-stones and for homes, for sisters and
  for wives,
For State-Rights and for honor, they stake their
  names and lives;
For the Hero-days of Old, when their dauntless
  Fathers stood;
For North Point's battle-field, and " McHenry
  stained in blood.

By all these potent memories, to nerve our strong
   right arms ;

By every manly instinct, that Southern courage
   warms ;

On sacred soil we 'll meet the foe, *nor trust for
   Peace to words* —

But test our rights as freeman — at the points of
   gleaming swords.

BALTIMORE, APRIL 21st, 1861.

AN INVOCATION.

Oh, save from fratricidal strains
　The hard right hands of those who go,
With banded armies' bristling trains
　And War's concomitants of woe;
　Where Rapine lurks and torches glow.

Oh, stand in might between the brave,
　To curb their frenzy!　Raise Thy arm,
In mercy, clothed with power to save!
　Let Reason ring the first alarm,
　And Peace avert the threatening storm.

Begin the war — and for all time
　The record of disgrace shall stand;
A glaring page of blood and crime,
　A burning stain of darkest brand,
　A blighting curse upon the land,

A by-word of contempt with men;
  "Till marked throughout the world with
    scorn,
They 'll point in mock'ry at us then,
  Our banners prostrate, soil'd and torn;
  Of prestige robbed, of honor shorn.

Extend, Oh Lord, thy saving arm,
  And grant that Peace her wings expand,
To shield us from the fierce alarm;
  Ere flaming torch, and gleaming brand
  Shall desolate a once blest land.

ANNAPOLIS JAIL, May 26, 1861.

A PRISONER OF WAR.

TO AN OLD PORTRAIT.

In dingy frame all dark with mould,
    Tho' stains and damp its tints efface,
A portrait — stern, and grim and old,
    The type of a determined race.
With calm blue eye, 'neath frowning brow
    Where earnest thoughts wove lines of care
Deep furrowed by the driving plow
    Of Time, that furrows everywhere.
With iron jaw and lip compressed ;
    With ragged beard, all streak'd with gray ;
A noble face but grief oppressed —
    A Puritan of Cromwell's day.

Say soldier of the olden time
    As now from out thy rusted frame
Thou lookest in this Western clime
    On fratricidal war and shame ;

Are these descendants of thy stock,
　Who rule the land with iron rod,
Such men as first found Plymouth Rock,
　And landed there to worship God?
Is this the home where first they raised,
　Their temples by the sounding sea;
Where first their guileless children praised
　The God who taught them to be free?
Are these, who stain the South with gore
　Regardless of the Wrong or Right,
Such men as in the "days of yore,"
　Had braved a boasting tyrant's might.

Blush, Soldier, in your dingy frame,
　And pray that time and damp may hide
Each feature, as is hid your name,
　While such inhuman deeds abide;
And intercede before that throne,
　Where Puritans were wont to bow,
For wisdom — as in old days shown —
　To those who rule the nation now.

August, 1862.

CHARADE.

Virginia's stronghold, wild and steep;
Where Shenandoah's waters leap
    To join Potomac's flood.
'Neath craggy mount, through rocky dell,
The River's rushing torrents swell;
    'T was there my first drank blood
Of brethren slain — "to save the Right."
Far better saved by vote than fight,
    Though bravely both sides stood.

Where Bull Run's sluggish waters glide,
The rebel army's horsemen ride
    Across the battle-field;
By hill, and vale, and clump of wood,

In serried ranks batallions stood,
   Half-hid, and half-revealed.
Behind my Second, close arrayed,
With neither flag nor gun displayed,
   His men were all concealed.
My whole, there gained the honored name
That through the valley blazed like flame
   Where'er his volleys pealed.

A PRISONER,

(ON RECEIVING FLOWERS FROM HOME.)

As welcome symbols of the loved ye come
  To cheer the gloom that hangs about this cell,
Laden with odors of the far-off home
  The brown leafed shrub, the lily's bell,
  And crimson rose, with fragrant smell.

Fresh in your various tints as when
  Were first unfolded to the morning light,
On hill-side green, or in the woodland glen,
  Those trembling petals, rich and bright,
  Enrobed in purple, pink and white.

Emblems of Hope, from her whose true heart
    sends,
  A love light to his gloomy prison's shade ;
Whose pure devotion, to her husband lends
  New strength to every firm resolve he made,
  To wield in Sacred Cause, a soldier's blade.

ANNAPOLIS JAIL, June 2, 1861.   A PRISONER OF WAR.

PAST, PRESENT AND FUTURE,

OF 1862.

In the dim vista of the Past appears
  A lengthened file in long procession's line;
The hero-statesmen of the by-gone years
  Whose noble names all noble hearts enshrine.

Look to the Present, and in contrast see
  A Nation's struggle, unexcused by fame;
A Nation's folly, where it should be free,
  A Nation's discord, leading on to shame.

In the near future — God alone can tell
  What record to the world shall then be shown;
Perchance the Union, that we loved so well,
  By frantic factions to the wild-winds strown —
  And Freedom crouching at some tyrant's
  throne.

MOUNT VERNON,

On Hearing the Steamboat Bell Toll while Passing.

Back — ninety years on History's page,
    And when the Nation's life was young,
When men there were, both brave and sage,
    Whose deeds and names have since been sung.
Men of a stamp whose honor stands
    In contrast to the *custom* now ;
Men of purer lives and stainless hands
    With truth's impress on heart and brow ;
One sacred name "led all the rest : "
    On tented field, 'mid battle's brunt,
When 'ere the serried squadrons pressed
    His victor' helm was " at the front."
From Halls of State, sedate and wise,
    In after days when peace was won,
His fame ascended to the skies,
    And Heaven had claimed its Washington.

His dust now lies beneath the mound,
  That rises by Potomac's Shore;
Too lately shaken by the sound,
  Of battle's crash and cannon roar;
But could that dust have risen then
  And have resumed his living form,
To martial into ranks the men,
  Whose peerless valor braved the storm
We would not be what now we are;
  We should not see what since we've seen,
But, risen from successful war,
  Virginia's fields would all be green.
Virginia's sons again may shake
  Her grand old banners to the breeze;
"Sic Semper" yet again may wake
  Wild echoes over Southern leas.

    Toll, Toll the bells,
      As the boats pass by:
    Toll, Toll the bells,
      For the soul on high.

Each Southern heart at the solemn sound,
  Its homage yields to the sainted dead,
While mournful memories cluster round
  The shores where patriot blood was shed.

And spirits of the good and brave
  Who died defending " Sacred right,"
Keep silent watch around the grave ;
  And shadowy forms at dim twilight
Of fair-haired boys and stalwart men,
  With tattered garb and hungry eyes,
Still march by hill, and glade, and glen,
  And gather there in wild surprise.
They guard the grave.—They wait the hour
  Their sons and kinsmen to inspire,
When once again in steadfast power
  The Southern heart shall throb with fire.

And when in after years the bell
  Of passing steamer still shall toll,
And echoes on the breezes swell
  And o'er the placid waters roll,

The brave sons of those martyred dead
   Shall bend in reverence at the sound,
For Time's soft radiance still shall shed
   Its lustre o'er that hallowed ground.

SEPTEMBER 4th, 1873.

ELECTION ODE. [3]

.

Rouse for the battle, Freemen brave!
  Your Country calls for each man's aid,
Rouse, Freemen! by your votes to save
  The heritage your father's gave;
In wisdom bought — by valor paid.

  Rouse in your might! Let Honor stand
The beacon light to guide your choice;
  And echoes, over sea and land,
From Western mound to Eastern strand,
  Shall answer to your voice.

Triumphant through the land shall sweep —
  To-morrow — to the end of time —
The name of him you choose to keep
From factions dark, from treasons deep,
  That heritage sublime.

SPIRIT LAND.

When Death shall sever earthly ties
    And human forms decay,
There is a land beyond the skies,
    Where happy spirits stray.

There in the realms where angels are,
    Again our souls shall meet;
Beneath the gleam of many a star
    My soul thy souls shall greet.

There, faithful to the vows we made
    With every action free,
In spirit robes of light array'd
    My love shall come to me;

Shall come, with dancing, joy-lit eye,
    With soft, wide open arms;
Shall come, in spirit-ecstasy,
    Clothed in immortal charms.

Blest, as They only there can bless,
  In purified desire ;
Where every Spirit-love's caress
  Burns with immortal fire.

Why chafe at human bonds with this
  The promise to thy fate ?
Why mourn at present ills, if bliss
  Makes glad thy future state?

Bear with the fleeting pangs of earth ;
  Nor shrink beneath the band ;
Thy solace is the happy birth
  In promised Spirit Land.

IN MEMORIAM. [4]

The Almighty's voice hath called thee
   From paths where virtues shine!
While mortal chains enthrall'd thee,
   Strong will and power were thine;
Performing man's best duties
   With a faith almost divine.

In the Temple's Halls a priest,
   High Priest, of brothers true;
In the battle where the least
   And the greatest look to you
As a warrior brave and noble,
   Whose faults in life were few.

In manhood's prime and power,
   Grand, vigorous and brave;

Responsive in the testing hour
　　When friendship's hand could save,
God called you to your home —
　　You found it — through the grave.

With drooping, tearful eyes,
　　Beside thy bier we stand;
Nor grief, nor human sighs,
　　Can break the endless band
Which heaven hath round thee cast,
　　And bound, with righteous hand.

LINES TO A LADY.

Like bright beams of sunshine illuming the moun-
    tain,
  When the green robe of Summer is worn by the
    earth,
Like spray-drops that glisten and shine from the
    fountain,
  Where brilliantly beautiful colors have birth ;

Like sweet songs of birds, in the close twining
    bowers
  Where beauty delights to hold her parterre,
Like delicate perfumes from ruby lipped flowers,
  Which were culled, little lady, to braid in thy
    hair.

Like moonbeams of silver and gold softly blending,
  Where angel-wing'd Zephyrs, with pinions out-
      spread,
Float over the edges of fleecy clouds, ending
  In the pure perfect blue of the ether o'er head;

Is thy love lighted presence in purity beaming
  With innocent mirth of the spirits sweet play
Resistless, with womanly witchery gleaming
  In radiant beauty's unconscious array.

For genius shines in those brown eyes bright glances,
  While pride sits in State on the classical brow ;
And the voice, in its tone of persuasion entrances —
  Methinks that the echoes are vibrating now.

In worth as in beauty, unrivalled, unmatched,
  Each exquisite feature adorned by a grace:
For the light of a sunbeam, in truant play catched,
  Was stolen to linger and shine on that face.

FLOWERS.

(ENCLOSED FROM HOME, TIED WITH WIFE'S HAIR.)

Wild-wood Flowers, of perfume sweet,
Love's messengers, my love to greet,
   You send me, " Katie," when you write :
Flowers that bloomed beside the spring,
   With waters dancing in the light ;
Flowers, whose modest blossoming
   My darling to the dells invite.

Bright leafed flowers, whose fresh tints come
As emblems of our joys at home ;
   Pure in their beauties from the hand
Whose every gift to man is good ;
   Nursed by Spring, whose breath had fann'd
With Zephyrs soft, each hill and wood ;
   In verdure clad, where winter stood.

Fragrant flowers, of varied hue;
The modest violet's purpled blue,　　·
　　Hearts-ease, prompting thoughts of love,
And lilies, with their drooping heads,
　　As list'ning to bird-songs above,
From where the branching tree-top spreads:
And crimson woodbine's slender threads.

Tied with thy hair.　Its ebon braid,
Where oft and oft my hand has laid,
　　Now binds the stems in close embrace;
And binds them, as thy love binds me,
　　In bonds of beauty, worth and grace;
Bonds, from which I could not be
By worlds of other love set free.

PRAYER OF THE TEMPTED.

Oh heart, that loves too well,
Oh lip, I fondly press,
Oh passion's burning swell,
That comes with his caress;
Oh strange magnetic force,
That sways my yielding will;
Oh soft, beguiling voice,
Seductive in its thrill;
Oh earnest, truthful eye,
Oh sweet, enticing smile,
Oh clasp, in which I lie;
Can love like this be guile?

Oh sin! for by such name
The world would call these bonds,

And brand me with a shame
  To which my pride responds;
Oh Time! has thou no balm,
  No solace, for such pain?
Oh Storm! will come no calm,
  No freedom from this chain?

Oh God! will thou not hear
  The prayer my heart sends up?
Will not Thy mercy spare
  My lip, "this bitter cup?"
Oh help me then to crush
  This wild entrancing pain,
Whose fatal surges rush,
  Resistless as the main,
Remorseless as the sea,
  With death on ev'ry wave;
Is there no mortal plea
  A sinking soul to save?

AUTUMN'S EVE.

Autumn has come with shadowy pall,
   With misty skies of softer blue,
With quivering leaves, that silent fall,
   Of Scarlet tints and golden hue.

The western clouds still wear the tinge
   That Summer's gorgeous sunsets wore;
But edged with borders of paler fringe
   Than sunset clouds of Summer bore.

The evening star, with calm cold light,
   Shines with a clearer, brighter beam,
As roll the deepening shades of night
   In sombre folds o'er hill and stream.

The young moon sinking down to rest,
   When days last gleam has almost gone ;

With chasten'd glitter lights the west
  Where sunset's beauties lately shone.

The fairest scene that Nature's brow,
  With shining coronet displays ;
Is Autumn's evening's fading glow,
  Adorned by crescent moonlight rays.

PARTINGS.

The ivy to the strong oak clings
  With many a twining tendril's hold ;
While dense festoons in dark green rings
  In close embrace each branch enfold.
Should lightning rend the rugged oak.
The clinging ivy shares the stroke :
  So woman's pure devotion shares
    With him, round whom her love's entwin'd,
  The joy, the sorrow, and the cares
    Which on life's pathway they may find ;
'Till death's rude hand the bond hath broke ;
More cruel than the lightning stroke.
  One heart survives to suffer still
    In grief, from bitter partings pangs ;
  Dark grief, whose cup sad memories fill,
    While o'er her soul a presence hangs.

The maiden when, with many a sigh,
  She marks that distant ship that bears
Her sailor love, with tearful eye
  And soul oppressed with doubt and fears;
Hath faith that, when the year rolls round
Her conscious heart with joy will bound
    In gladdening welcome sweet and pure;
      And angels whisper, in her dreams,
    Of other joys, unknown before,
      Whose presence in his coming gleams.
But storms, where terror's rage and rave,
May sink that ship beneath the wave;
  And dreams, that tranquil slumbers weave,
    When Love and Hope bright promise shed,
  May glad those slumbers, to deceive,
    And gild the pall that Fate hath spread.

The mother, when she gives her son
  To battle for his country's fame,
And stakes his life where glory 's won,
  'Mid sabre-stroke and cannon flame,
  Hopes with a mothers faith and pride.

That, 'mongst the great and good and brave,
  His name may shine with bright names there,
  If sacrificed " The Right" to save ;
   And Heaven-ward sends her trembling prayer
That God her noble boy will guard,
And bless her with the sweet reward
   Again his living form to hold
    In safety to her beating heart ;
   In conscious pride that brave and bold
    He bore a christian soldier's part.
But while her prayer ascends to God
   His form may welter on the sod ;
For forms as fair, and young, and brave,
Have filled a martyred soldier's grave.

WOULDST THOU FORGET?

Could fabled Lethe's waters drown
　　The memory of the by-gone day,
And darkness o'er the Past be thrown,
　　Illumined by no single ray
Of all that soul-entrancing time,
　　When first our hearts responsive beat,
Like rich toned bells, at Easter chime,
　　In soft accord, and passing sweet ;
Wouldst Thou, my love of all those years,
　　The waters quaff, and thus forget
An image, that thy heart declares
　　Enshrined in secret worship yet ?
An image, bound by many a chain ;
　　A sainted idol, dear and blest.
Oh, better far the love retain,
　　That stood such hard abiding test,
Than seek to drown in Lethe's wave
　　A tie that time has failed to sever ;
Which, destined to outlive the grave,
　　Shall bloom in Spirit land forever.

ERIN.

There's an Isle in the Ocean, whose sons are as
    brave
As the Heroes of Old, in whose fame we delight;
With hearts wild and free as the foam-crested wave
    That breaks on her shores, in its grandeur and
    might.

Where the spirit of Freedom, 'ere-while has been
    nursed,
    Where the martyrs of Liberty died in their gore,
Where the tyrants who bind her will ever be cursed,
    Till Tyranny holds her in thraldom no more.

'T is the Green Isle of Erin, bowed down by the
    might
    Of the Sister, who rears her proud crest o'er the
    sea ;
But the glad day shall come, when her sons, in the
    fight,
    Shall have proved their Green Island — The Isle
    of the Free.

THE SHIPWRECK. [5]

I.

A stifling Summer's noonday heat
  Glares on the Mart of Trade,
As earnest groups pass down a street
  To the docks where ships are laid;
And gather for a sad farewell,
  Perhaps the last in life,
To some, who tempting ocean's swell,
  'Mid raging Storm-wind's strife,
Seek distant shores, for wealth and ease,
Adown the paths of the " sounding seas."

A proud ship at her anchor rides,
Brave men throng her graceful sides,
  And gentle woman too is there;
  Full many a pleading look and prayer
  To Heaven ascends; and many a tear
On many a cheek abides.

II.

The whispered word, the smothered sigh,
　　The touch of lips no more to meet,
The love-look in the glistening eye,
　　The lingering parting, sadly sweet.
Friends, Country, Home, to memory dear,
　　When backward wandering thought will stray:
We leave them heart oppressed by fear,
　　We leave them — and they pass away.

　　　They pass, as down the stream we glide,
　　. But Courage stems the troubled tide;
　　　And high before him Hope holds up,
　　　With promise brimmed, her golden cup;
　　　For Hope is Youth's fair bride.

III.

Out in the stream ! with white sails bent,
　　The ship moves slowly from the land;
And echoing farewell shouts are sent
　　And many a parting wave of hand —

But soon grows dim the distant shore
    Beneath the lingering sunset's ray,
And homes now left for ever more
    Are fading with the dying day.

    While rippling waves their spray drops throw,
    All sparkling with reflected glow,
        The ship is dashing through the sea,
        Her stalwart sailors, bold and free,
        Move on her decks right merrily —
    And joy is at the flow.

IV.

A clipper ship, whose sharp lined prow
    A wondrous speed betokens well;
From keel to capstan, stern to bow,
    All shaped in lines of graceful swell;
Her yards wide reach beyond her beams,
    With snowy canvass squarely spread;
A living thing at sea she seems
    With light clouds floating overhead.

Her tall masts reaching up and high,
From which her pennants proudly fly
  And with the fleecy cloud flakes flirt;
  With many a strand of rigging girt,
  She braveth every harm and hurt
    From stormy sea and sky.

V.

Far out upon the mighty deep,
  In paths beyond the reach of aid,
Where roaring billows grandly sweep
  Her beauties are displayed;
As bending to the freshening gales
  'Mid seas where gulls and dolphins sport,
With freight of lives and wealth she sails,
  For shores where lie her destined port.

  But soon the baffling breeze comes warm
  From fragrant flowers of graceful form,
    Its breath all laden with perfume
    Of climes which Southern suns illume;
    While lurking terrors, dark with gloom
      Portend a Tropic storm.

VI.

Upon her crowded decks a throng,
    That counts at least two hundred souls:
To some the weary voyage seems long,
    Some lounge and watch old ocean's rolls,
Some bask beneath the sails' deep shade
    In fancy wandering far away.
Fair visions those — with Hope arrayed
    In Fortune's glitter in the distant day.

    In contrast there, the men, her crew,
    Of stalwart forms — brave hearts and true —
        In Danger's storm-rocked cradle nursed;
        Their songs upon the sea air burst
        Daring the winds to do their worst,
            As o'er the waves she flew.

VII.

After a sun bright Tropic day
    The shades of night come down a pace,
And cloud banks force their shadowy way
    Across the far horizon's face :

The Western sky, with sunset red,
    Is gathering in a gloomy frown,
"Till far and near and over spread
    A grayish, leaden pall hang down.

    "T is calm! No sound disturbs the deep,
    No breezes o'er its surface sweep,
        No motion tells of latent life,
        But tokens of dark terrors rife,
        And omens of the coming strife
            Are in that treacherous sleep.

VIII.

Now distant thunders low and hoarse
    Athwart the Firmament have passed;
The ship is drifting from her course,
    Her sails flap loosely from the mast;   ·
And hearts that heretofore were bold
    Are trembling with a nameless fear,
As many a shipwreck's tale is told
    To vibrate on the listener's ear.

Come memories of the long-loved home,
And crowding thoughts, in swift array.
Of joys or sins of the by-gone day,
In rapid retrospective play,
Flash like the ocean foam.

IX.

Hark, to the wild resistless rush
Of waters in their noisy might ;
And foam capped waves, with brilliant flush
Of phosphorescent rays of light,
Are gliding onward, courser like,
With loose manes tossed erect and free,
And blasts of wind in fury strike
At intervals, the seething sea.

The clouds have gathered in the North !
The Storm-King brings his chariot forth ;
While vivid lightning gleam on high
His courses start, with radiant eye,
Before the hurricane they fly
Swift o'er the white sea's froth.

X.

Careening low before the blast,
 A ship all helpless in the storm;
With sails in tattered fragments cast,
 With strained and quivering form.
The Ocean's frown grows darker yet,
 The Ocean demons claim their prey,
Upon her doom a seal is set,
 Her guardian angels — where are they?

Go ask of the loudly echoing gale
That tore in shreds her snow white sail;
 Or ask — pale lipped in mortal fear —
 Of the fiends that throng the stormy air,
 And the answer — that those echoes bear
 An agonizing wail!

XI.

On dreams of home their cold eyes close;
And the Shadow of Death in the storm arose;
 Terribly stern for the soul to see.
Oh where is the promise of wealth and ease;

Oh where are the hopes that Fancy please?
  All vanished with the mysteries
That Fate hath sunk in the fathomless seas!

For surging with a rushing sound,
The gallant ship a port hath found,
  Near by the Mermaid caves;
And the Billows, as they sweep along,
And the Winds, shall sing the funeral song
  Above those Ocean graves.

DREAMS.

Do dreams portray, distinct or dim,
  Prophetic scenes of joy or dread —
And come they in the guise of him,
  Whose love is round thy pathway spread?

If distant scenes of girl-hood's day
  Sometimes thy peaceful slumbers fill,
And tones of dear ones, far away,
  With almost real distinctness thrill —

If dream-land's scenes sometimes repeat
  The ardent glance, the burning kiss,
The firm tread of the echoing feet,
  Of him with whom you share your bliss —

Are all your dreams of pleasant shade,
   Of rosy hues, of happy hours,
Of sunshine, and in light arrayed;
   Are all your visions crowned with flowers?

If some sad dream thy slumbers break,
   In which a well-loved form is seen,
Should dream-clad phantoms' semblance shake
   Such faith as yours has always been?

A VALENTINE.

(WRITTEN FOR A GAY OLD FRIEND.)

Some twenty years or more ago,
  When you and I were young and gay,
'Mid wild New Hampshire's hills of snow —
  'T was on a frost crisped winter day,
  That cuddled in a fur-wrapped sleigh
  We worshiped old St. Valentine.
How bright your eyes, your voice how low
  And sweet to words I whispered then ;
    And how your hand clasp answered mine ;
    Two votaries at Young Love's shrine,
  As we dashed gaily down the glen.

Those days were glad, and years have flown,
While other joys our hearts have known,
  And other ties around us thrown.

But much I doubt if since that ride,

By memory drifted down the tide

Where Youth is wrecked, one single gleam

So bright has glistened o'er the stream ;

Tho' surely Peace hath blessed us both ;

And now sedately, I may send

In lines where love and honor blend,

Not emphasized by pledge or oath,

A simple greeting, kind and pure,

In tribute to those " days of yore ;"

And pledge thy health in rich red wine,

My darling Old-Time Valentine.

PASSION.

In human hearts wild passions blaze
  With fierce volcanic fires;
While fervent Youth her bloom displays
  All warm with soft desires.

No mortal skill the ship can save
  Disabled in the storm,
Where Ocean's wild, resistless wave
  Engulphs its shattered form.

No human hand the silken car
  Can guide, in mid-air's path;
Relentless winds, at constant war,
  May crush it in their wrath.

No mortal will the dread decree
Of Death may turn aside;
Or solve Creation's mystery,
That all who lived, have died.

Nor human will can passions tame
Except by faith and prayer,
In Him and to His holy name,
Who placed those passions there.

TIME.

Time moves along
On sluggish wing;
A mournful song
Its phantoms sing.

In sorrowing cadence fall
The plaintive notes of woe;
With strange, entrancing thrall
Its measured anthems flow,
When strains of pleasures past,
Of hours of fleeting bliss,
Vibrate, in strong contrast
To gloomy hours, like this.
For joy no more can wake
The heart whose Hopes lie dead,
Or from its banner shake
The dust which time hath spread.

The hours have left the moth
  Whose brilliant tints have been,
'Till now, no more the cloth
  Is bright with gold and green,
Unfurl the banner then
  To find its hues effaced ;
Unmask the hearts of men
  And see what Time has traced.

  Time moves along
    On sluggish wing,
  A mournful song
    Its phantoms sing.

CLOUDS. (6)

The clouds upon their sky —
Separation's pangs and loneliness to each ;
Nor doth their reason resignation teach ;
The hours of absence marked by many a sigh.
The dead Past's memories from out the gloom,
Rise, phantom like as from the silent tomb,
  And, voiceless, pass them by.

The clouds upon their hearts —
What was pleasing then, retains some freshness yet,
The faith then pledged, is kept to-day as well,
Still smile meets-smile, still strange pulsations
  swell,
With ardor fierce as when in youth they met :
But ties they dreamed not then, are woven now ;
The stamp of Time hath deeply marked each
  brow ;
While stings of Care have left their burning smarts
Will sunlight ever dawn upon their hearts ?

Whence come these clouds, this storm ?
From Fate's decree that parted thus their lives —
   Are they yet so young, that passions warm
And follies still pursue them on their path,
To hang about them in dark shapes of wrath,
   Against which each too feebly strives ;
For since like theirs a half repentance were in vain ;
It would but serve to forge, in stronger links the
    chain —
Such cloud as these bring lightning with their rain !

IN ABSENCE.

I am sad to-night and cursing fate,
  In my chamber, all alone ;
The clock struck six, and seven, and eight,
  And the dreary hours wear on.

Silent and sad in the dull cold room,
  No smile, no touch, no sound ;
No loved one's presence to break the gloom
  Of the four white wall's chill bound.

The city noises all are hushed
  Save the sound of the fireman's call,
And of rolling wheels as engine rushed
  Where burning rafters fall.

Or of some one late, the heavy tread,
　　Uncertainly staggering home,
With throbbing pulse and aching head,
　　From the wine cup's sparkling foam.

Or moaning wind in the house's eaves,
　　Singing a dirge, perhaps;
Or stealthy tread of mid-night thieves,
　　Or spirits mysterious raps.

These are the sounds which weave a spell,
　　Of gloomy and mystical power;
These, and the tongue of the vibrating bell
　　That is tolling the mid-night hour.

Sounds of the night — startling and wierd —
　　Sounds that but darkness hath had;
Sounds that the pinions of Silence have stirr'd—
　　Dreary, monotonous sad.

IN " A. M's" ALBUM.

As flows the streamlet to the river,
Laughing riplets on its face
In the sunlight dance and quiver,
Ceaseless in their endless race ;
Even so, in charming grace,
Maiden fancies form and flow ;
Ardent, truthful, hopeful, pure,
Never fearing once the river,
Never shrinking from the shore.

A THOUGHT.

Should life be measured by years,
  Or rather by what we have seen?
Tho' snow with the winter appears,
  The grass underneath may be green.

Doth passion with youth all expire,
  Or rather lie dormant and tame?
Tho' ashes may smother the fire,
  It waits but to burst into flame.

Why then should we ever grow old,
  Why mourn over joys that have gone,
If love that we cherished grows cold
  New love in the morrow may dawn.

LINES OF THE "LONG AGO."

When morning's blush first gilds with rosy hue,
  Mountain and vale and Ocean's breast;
'Ere rising Phœbus' rays disperse the blue
  Pale mist which on the hill tops rest;
Lost in reflection sweet I wander forth,
  To dream of thee and muse upon thy worth.

No pagan idol on a Hindoo shrine,
  Nor golden image of the Aztec creed,
Receives such homage as is justly thine,
  For maiden beauty's matchless meed.
Happy the man on whom thy smiles descends,
  On only one its tranquil beams may light;
Where Youth to Love a glamor lends,
  It charms to worship and to pure delight.

ENIGMA.

My first, is always made to keep
   The tide or stream within due bound;
My second, on the rolling sweep
   Of everlasting Time is found.

My first, a safeguard is, if strong;
   Becomes a curse by adding " n ";
My second, feebly moving on,
   Is always deemed a curse by men

My whole, if weak or frail my first,
   The consequence would be,
Should tide, or stream, their bondage burst,
   And sweep the fabric toward the sea.

CHARADE.

From the first feeble lisp with which infancy strives
  Its wants to express or affection display,
To the time when the Death Angel's summons ar-
    rives
  And the aims of a lifetime are passing away,
My first must be used by child and by sage
  In simple expression or eloquent speech;
On the record of progress, adorning the page,
  By prelates, expounding the creed that they
    preach:
The learned, must use it in prose and in verse,
The wicked, may use it for purposes worse.

My second denotes what the honest and true
  From public opinion receive as their meed;
A word which when spoken as justly the due
  Of the good, is a tribute of honor indeed.

The value of all that we buy it defines;
  From the house where we live and the garments
    we wear,
To the gold in the mint, and the ore at the mines,
  To the fish of the sea, and the birds of the air;
The wordly, must win it by barter and gain.
The worthy, may win it through hardship and pain.

  A poet's name my whole discloses,
    Whose verses pure shall live through ages,
  In lines so sweet, that Spring's first roses
    Seem scattered o'er his varied pages.

INDIAN FUNERAL IN MEXICO.[7]

Behind the western mountain's brow,
The wearied Sun is sinking low
    And night's deep shades
Will soon beneath her mantle hide
The distant village, steep hill-side
    And verdant glades.

'Mid Southern climes and near a spring,
Whose flower clad banks a perfume fling,
    So soft and pure,
Upon the slumbering evening air,
That tardy Twilight lingers there
    At day's closed door.

A toil stained band of rugged men
Have camped within the silent glen
    Beside the stream,
Where moonlight through the foliage plays,
'Mid pale, dim stars, with fitful rays
    And wavering gleam.

As slowly wear the hours of night
Close by their watch-fire's smothered light
    They lay around,
Those wearied men, in slumber lost,
While dreams — perchance of danger -— tost
    Their rest profound.

Mayhap to some, down Memory's steep
The rushing tide of home-thoughts sweep,
    And faces fair,
With radiant smiles of greeting glad.
In vision's joyous fancies clad,
    Again are near.

Mayhap of love one's voice the tone
Across the reach of Time is thrown
     And softens sleep —
But Hark! The pilgrims' dreams are broke —
No voice of loved one softly woke
     Their slumbers deep ;

But murmured sounds that gently move
The echoes of the leafy grove
     Are borne along;
A saddened cadence marks the notes,
In melancholy music floats
     The dirge-like song.

With slowly measured, heavy tread
The funeral bearers of the dead
     In gloom appear,
Like phantom forms with gestured weird,
And shrieks and shouts, in discord heard,
     Inspiring fear.

Close 'mid their ranks they bear the form
Of one whose manly heart beat warm
    With kindred throes;
And march with solemn dirge and tear
And Pagan rites to guard his bier
    To death's repose —

Of one of noble Indian race,
  Who, sire and son, with Aztec race
    Of royal blood,
Their mighty ancestry still mourn,
From splendor by the Spaniard torn
    Mid'st fire and flood.

Or, of some maiden, darkly bright,
With lip of coral, hair of night
    And dusky hue;
Whose veins were charged with blood too
    warm,
Whose heart had beat, in Passion's storm,
    With throb too true.

Delusion strange, their custom seems
Like fantasies of fevered dreams
    That darkly roll;
The frantic dread that demon force
May wrest away the loved one's corse,
    May seize his soul;

The mystic faith that shout and song,
Whose echoes night winds waft along,
    Will demons fright —
But safe the form beneath the sod
The soul, reclaimed, returns to God
    In raiment bright. . .

In the deep gloom the train moved on —
When every measured tread had gone,
    'Mid Quiet's reign,
Beside their watch-fire's smouldering ray,
The weary, startled pilgrims lay
    In rest again.

WAITING.

Waiting for Life — where the germ has been sown
   By the boisterous wind, on its wandering way:
The seed that its pinions have scattered and strown,
   Tho' they spring into life, shall fade and decay.

Waiting for Youth—how each boy counts the hours,
   That yet must elapse 'ere his childhood has
      passed;
And anxiously longing, in Fancy, devours
   The joyful fruition of manhood's repast.

Waiting for Love — that his young heart had
      cherished;
   His visions of sleep had pictured its charms;
Still waiting—'till Faith in its object had perished,
   'Neath Jealousy's blight, or Inconstancy's storms.

Waiting for Fame—where the war-trumpet's sound,
   And the tramp of mailed squadrons are shaking
      the plain ;
Where the dead and the dying are scattered around,
   And missiles fall thick as the Equinox rain.

Waiting for Death — on that stern field of glory ;
   And wounded to death, while waiting for fame ;
An exemplified proof, that in truth as in story,
   The lustre reflects, not from deeds, but their
      name.

HOPE.

Of Hope and her visions I write
   While her beautiful wings unclose,
With plumage effulgently bright,
In a sort of electrical light,
   Reflected from Promise, its glows
   With tints of the *couleur de rose.*

When Youth sends his bark on the stream,
   All freighted with joys that elate,
The after years shine with a gleam
   That defies the stern warnings of Fate;
For down, where the smooth current flows,
Is reflected the *couleur de rose.*

When Sorrows surround us with shade,
   When Want casts her mantle of gloom,

When Friendship and Love are betrayed
 And the heart looks for rest to the tomb,
Then Hope to the future out-throws
Her banner of *couleur de rose*,

But should the dark portents prove true
 And Death come while Sorrows abide,
In Heaven's cerulean blue
 Our hopes o'er the billows shall ride:
And there in that land shall repose
'That bloometh in *couleur de rose.*

HAPPINESS.

Thou phantom Happiness! Thou mortal boast!
  Thou shadow! men pursue through all life's
    gloom;
Which, 'mongst the winding paths where peace is
    lost,
  Will best prepare thy pilgrims for the tomb?

Not thine unhappy Love — with faltering tone,
  And eye upturned to meet the glance of her
Whose smile enraptures, should its charm be thrown
  On him, the Angel-woman's worshiper.

Not thine Ambition — grasping lust for fame;
  With deep marked foot-prints, stamped in human
    gore;
And fading trophies scarred by crime and shame;
  While stings of conscience rankle in the sore.

Nor Miser, thine—with maddening thirst for gold;
　The one absorbing passion of thy brain;
Were thine such hoards as Crœsus had of old,
　Their still would rule the insatiate greed of gain.

But thine, pure Christian — steadfast, true and
　　brave;
　Above all selfish aims thy motives soar;
With firm conviction in *His* power to save;
　Nor wasting life on Love, nor Wealth, nor War.

Thine is the goal, at which all men have aimed;
　Thine is the boast, and thine the one true road;
Thine is the charm, from mortal passions tamed;
　And thine is Happiness — through Faith in God.

COMPENSATION.

The tree that bends before the blast,
    Recoils again and stands upright;
And when the Summer storm has passed
    Its leaves shall glitter in the light.
The heart bowed down with grief to-day,
    To-morrow may new bliss enjoy ;
No distant sorrows, dim and gray,
    That heart's enchantment shall destroy,
The storms of life, when stern and dark
    The Present to the soul may seem ;
(As on some stranded shipwrecked bark,
    Adrift upon Fate's tide or stream)
What though the surges darkly frown,
    And o'er the shattered wreck may roll,
For Mercy, with her shining crown,
    And hand that grasps a stainless scroll,

From Heaven, above, is looking down
   To save from wreck a human soul.
A legend on that scroll is seen,
   Which since Creation's day hath stood ;
When first, 'midst Eden's groves, serene,
The God of Mercy spake it —" Good."

LINES WITH A RING.

Accept this ring dear girl and think
    Of what was told you long ago ;
The stone it holds is topaz pink
    And will become that hand of snow,
Refuse it not, for Fate decreed
    Thou should'st receive a golden token ;
So let this little emblem plead,
    An advocate of love unspoken.

DOUBT.

You say you love me, yet you leave me now,
  Alone and wearied, aimless and distressed ;
You, faithless to your every pledge and vow,
  And I, too constant, find you like the rest.
Some other love may cheer your future path,
  But will that love be half so true as mine ?
And in that future, will no memory's wrath,
  In terror, rise to scare you from the shrine?
But when at last, beneath the church-yard sod,
  At rest from all these cares, we both shall lie :
And when the record shall be called by God,
  And we shall stand for judgment — You and I —
Who at the throne shall then seem least to blame
  For all these wrongs from which we suffer now?
Who caused the sorrow — and on whom the shame?
  Who then shall answer for each broken vow?
Well ! the illusion of the dream has passed ;
  The tasted joys are only Dead-Sea fruit ;
And 'midst the darkness that this grief has cast
  The very pulses of my heart are mute.

SOLACE.

Joy! for she comes, to pledge and promise true;
   The doubts were only fond love's foolish pain;
She comes and tells me —" If I only knew
   The struggles that were made to break the chain;
The pangs they cost, the dreary sleepless nights,
   The lonely days of anxious wearying thought,
The fear, the dread and then the soft delights
   That dreams, persuasive, sometimes brought;
The pressing need in some one to confide;
   The wish, that burned but could not be confessed,
That ebbed and flowed resistless as the tide,
   By human will too strong to be repressed;
The apprehension that our love was crushed;
   That wrong and anger had its fervor chilled "—
But rose-hued Hope, with memory flushed,
   The bowl of Promise to the brim has filled;
And Love's red wine's intoxicating draught,
   Shall add to pleasures and their zest renew;
And when our lips in mutual love have quaffed
   The God-like nectar — She 'll believe me true.

THE SWITCH.

Said Harry to Jane one bright Summer day —
While engaged on the lawn at a game of croquet
And Jane's little head wore a chignon so grand
It had scarcely an equal for size in the land —
You 'll doubtless esteem me an impudent dog,
But why is your head like an old pedogogue
Whose greatest delights are to teach and to flog,
Pray tell me my dear where the likeness comes in ?
How the deuce should I know; She replied with a
    grin
And a glance with a glamour that savored of sin —
Well then tho' you charge me with insolent non-
    sense,
The size of its switch addeth much to its conse-
    quence.

CAUTIONS.

(DURING THE GOLD EXCITEMENT IN NEW YORK IN 1864.)

Seek not for wealth where gamblers meet
On shaded side of crowded street,
Noisy and rude, in clamorous greed,
As carrion birds in search of feed
    Where the battle has fiercest raged ?
Eager and anxious, pursuing the doom,
That, shadow-like, hangs about the room
Where gold is bartered and fortune marred,
More surely than by dice or card
In the fight with the " Tiger " waged.

Seek not for wealth where stocks are sold
At the " call of the Lists " — but not for gold :
" Promoters" grasp what profits are made
And men of mark are always paid
    For the prestige of their names ;

Unscrupulous, sordid, defrauding their friends,
Degrading themselves to infamous ends !
What matter the millions they dying may leave,
What matter the wealth their heirs may receive,
If burdened by similar shames ?

COURAGE.

Days, dark stormy days of gloom ;
　　Nights, long sleepless nights of thought ;
Constant cares, that peace consumes,
　　By every passing hour are brought,
Debt, the Demon, clanks a chain ;
　　Want, the spectre, standing near,
Surrounded by a shadowy train
　　Whose potent leader's name is Fear ;
In the distance angels hover,
　　Rays of light surround their forms,
Before them is a bridge that over
　　Courage strides and braves the storms ;
Faith beside him keeping pace,
　　Cheers him where the bridge is weak,
And Hope beyond, with smiling face,
　　But tears bedewing either cheek,
Still beckons from the angel throng,
　　That courage never once may falter ;
For though the bridge be steep and long,
　　Its distant end is Hope's bright altar.

FORGET THEE.

Forget Thee! Can the Earth forget to bear
Upon her bounteous bosom's emerald fields
Glad, golden harvests in return for warmth
Received from laughing Spring's embrace?

Forget Thee! Can the placid stream forget
In glittering radiance back to give
The beams upon her silvery surface cast
By the inconstant Harvest moon?

Forget Thee; Can the once rich man forget
The wealth, by hard, untiring toil obtained,
And prized so dearly that when it vanished,
He had well nigh died? Who still a weary,
Feeble, sad existence drags along,
In hope that yet his nerveless, palsied hand
Again may clutch his often counted gold.

Forget Thee? As well the martyred saint
When agonized and dying at the stake,
With trembling hands upraised, and eyes
To Heaven upturned, forget to call
For mercy and for strength upon his God!

PATIENCE.

When dews of night are lightly shed
Upon some fragile floweret's head,
   The stem beneath the dew will stand;
But under bursts of wind and rain,
The flower must break, nor rise again
   When sunshine lights the land.

So trials when they fall like dews,
New vigor to the heart infuse,
   Nor bend, nor break the stem;
But falling 'neath a storm of care,
And pressing round us everywhere;
   There is no shield from them.

They bend, they bow us to the ground;
We seldom rise with the rebound,
   Save by the force of will.
Some 'neath the storms of Life are brave
And wait 'till better fortunes save —
   But some are waiting still.

COLUMBUS.

" A Castilla y á Leon,
Nuevo Mundo dió Colon."

When from the Conquest of Granada the Queen of
Spain returned

And with glowing warlike ardor her knights and
soldiers burned ;

When the realm of Moorish power by Spanish arms
was crushed,

And through the story famed Alhambra the con-
quering thousands rushed ;

When mourned the Moorish Maidens their dusky
lovers slain,

And Christian knights were flushed with trophies
of the plain ;

When sad Boabdil's jeweled crown by Christian
hands was torn

From the Moslem chieftain's brow where so proudly it was worn ;   .

When the last of Moorish warriers had left the
worshiped shrines ;

Where the rose with jasmin flowers in fragrant
    grace entwines,
A careworn man, with saddened brow, to Isabel
    bent down,
With schemes of promised grandeur whose fame
    should grace her crown ;
With tales of distant lands, where constant sun-
    shine glows,
Where an eternal Spring-time, its ripening verdure
    throws ;
Where fruits of luscious sweetness, the tropic
    warmths repay,
And birds of gorgeous plumage, their feathered
    charms display ;
Where mines of untold golded wealth lie hid be-
    neath the soil —
And brilliant gems of priceless worth, are but the
    adventurer's spoil —
Beyond Atlantic's rolling tide, in the dim distance
    comes,
Before his seer-like vision a mighty Nation's
    homes:
With faith impressed and fervor he pleads his
    splendid scheme,
Till Isabel's proud heart believeth in his dream ;

And on her mind, in glory, breaks the dazzling
    future fame
That Time has yielded, treasure-like, in homage
    to her name —
Her royal jewels, prized and rich, were freely
    pledged and sold —
The purchase of a Western World, the Promised
    Land of Gold.

HOPE ON. [8]

God judgeth for the best;
Trust his wisdom for the rest;
Hopeful hearts are always blest;
    Hope On!

God guards the sparrow as it flies,
And his mercy never dies;
If on him thy trust relies,
    Hope On!

Be resigned, with humble heart;
Should he chasten, bear the smart,
Of Christian duty, 't is a part,
    Hope On!

If dark to-day, with grief and fear,
New light to-morrow : may appear;
Bend to God in humble prayer,

   Hope On !

Should his wisdom deem it best
To take him hence, to Heaven and rest;
Then thou 'lt know that he is blest.

   Hope On !

THE KNELL OF TIME.

(MID-NIGHT OF THE OLD YEAR.)

Hark to the tolling bell, that wakes the stillness of
  the night
With muffled, slow-toned music, for the year that's
  taking flight;
Down in the fathomless depths of Time, 'neath the
  waves of the boundless sea,

> Its grave is found
> Let the bell's deep sound
> Its parting requiem be.

No mourning train, with solemn pomp, its funeral
  pageant swells;
No mourning sound the silence breaks, save the
  sound of tolling bells;
But 'neath the gloom of midnight, the mourning
  pall is spread;

> The hour hath flown !
> Its days are done !
> Another year is dead.

FRAGMENT I.

For some have drank at Pleasure's Spring
  As though its waves could care assuage ;
But Love a funeral dirge would sing
  And Sorrow snatch from Memory's wing
A quill to blot Life's darkened page.

FRAGMENT II.

THE MAY-DAY PIC-NIC.

A quaint old house at the top of a hill
In the 'midst of a grove of grand old oaks :
Behind are dense thickets, where song birds trill,
And in front stands a cart with four oxen in yokes.
Round the house is a porch, with low hanging eaves,
With steps leading down to a beautiful lawn ;
And the twining clamatis, with petals and leaves,
Is shading the porch that its petals adorn.

An hundred years, or more, hath stood
That quaint old house — 'till bricks and wood
Are moulded and stained — 'neath roof and eave
Are nests of bats, and spiders weave
In fanciful webs their wonderful maps;
Themselves persuasively wonderful chaps.
Whose principal business is setting of trap.

Where innocent flies may meet with mishaps —
Much like to the traps gay gentlemen set
And bait with caresses and presents — " You bet "—
Some foolish young woman to coax to a net.

Ah! many the dance and wild carouse,
    When revels were kept in the days gone by,
In the halls of that singular quaint old house,
    And music and mirth were loud and high,
The women were fair as women are now ;
    The men were as brave, and gallant and gay ;
The wit was as pungent, and joyous the flow
    Of their pleasures, as those of their children
        to-day.

This morn, on the porch, are three sunny-faced
        girls,
    As full of their fun " as an egg is of meat;" ·-
Laughing and dancing, and tossing their curls,
    In a manner at once both provoking and sweet;
For these girls are determined on frolic and fun,
    Are bent on a May-day pic-nic spree.

And were rather impatiently waiting for one
  Who comes, and is welcomed with boisterous
    glee,
  For a marvelous fellow at frolics is he,
  He, and two others, as beaux for the three.

They 'd sent for the cart and oxen four,
Those three bright girls at the old house door:
And a more exquisite picture, I ween,
Was never before on that old porch seen,
      Than those three lasses,
      Of whom one wears glasses,
And of the beautiful trio is queen;
      But it must be confessed,
      If it 's not so, I 'll be — blessed,
That her air is more gay than serene.

      In all your excursions,
      Or foolish diversions,
Or among the acquaintances made in your lives,
Of maidens, or widows, or other men's wives,
      Have you even met one,
      Or desired to pet one,

Of those singular creatures
    Whose eyes were near-sighted ;
    And rather delighted
    To half close their lids
    While waiting for bids,
Distorting their features
    In a kind of a half quizical,
    Not at all metaphysical
    Sort of a glance,
Beneath which one almost drops off in a trance —
Because if you have you can understand why,
There's a magical witchery lurks in the eye
Of a near-sighted maiden, sedate and so shy,
And withall at the same time attractively sly —
So she, the bright queen of the aforementioned
    lasses,
To see at all clearly was compelled to wear glasses,
        And seemed much discreeter,
        And as decidedly sweeter,
As is best golden syrup than common molasses.

I neglected to say, in a casual way,

As I should — but my verses went slightly astray

The name of this near-sighted lady is Anna;

Her friends and respective associates Hannah,

And darling, diminutive, dainty, Diana.

But needing no further description just yet

> Than merely to tell

> That the last demoiselle.

Was 'mongst her acquaintances nick-named " The
Pet."

I said they 'd been waiting expecting their beaux,

  And mentioned the gentlemen too had arrived;

But some introduction, I rather suppose,

  Is requisite here if it can be contrived,

> Of the gentlemen three

> And especially he

Whose welcome was such, you might easily see

He was cock of the roost and a *rara avis.*

> There was Charley, the beau,

> John, rather slow,

And Robert, decidedly cockney, " you know."

Who dropping the " H " in speaking to Hannah,
T'was hard to decide if he meant her or Anna.

Now Charley, a reckless impetuous fellow,
　　At fox hunt or dinner,
Would sometimes get mellow ;
Addicted in fact to commit any sell, or
　　　　Practical joke on foe or on friend,
　　　　With or without either motive or end,
Was what might be termed a masculine sinner.
　　　Rakish his air and " devil may care,"
　　I believe in the French it is termed *debon-*
　　　　naire.
　　　　From the city had come,
　　　　And had not yet been home
From a very equivocal sort of a party,
Attractively made up of girls and écarté ;
And tainted somewhat with baccanal odor,
　　　Looked jaded and seedy
　　　As though he might need a
Matutinal drink of brandy and soda.

We most of us know, that after the flow

    Of the over-night wine, be it champagne or
      sherry,

    Has been kept up 'till morning in intercourse
      very

Delightfully charming, just while we were drinking,

    There's a penance to do, and a time to go through

    That's extremely distressing, at least while it's
      new,

And decidedly tends to institute thinking;

    A personal penalty paid for abuse,

And marked by some such annoying sensation

As head-ache or heart-burn, of which the relation

    Is almost too much for my muse.   *   *   *

FRAGMENT III. (9)

When night had cast her mantle o'er the earth,
And dreary darkness reigned, as at the birth
Of Light, from Chaos and confusion sprung;
And in the welkin dome bright stars were hung;
The pale Moon cast a weak and sickly shade,
As, scarce half-formed, she strove to light the glade;
While heavenly quiet reigned o'er all supreme,
(Fair Nature slumber'd, and enjoy'd her dream —)
A gloomy man, in restless, discontented mood,
Had wandered forth in solitude to brood
And impious questions raise 'gainst God, who made,
In wondrous beauty and in peace array'd,
A world for man and under his control,
But formed him subject to an immortal soul.

'Mid sins and wild excess his life had grown
'Till shattered Reason totter'd on her throne,

Like some huge rock, which long had stood secure
And firm, imbedded in the sandy shore,
Had brav'd the force that fiercest tempests flung,
By constant washing of the waves now hung
Almost without foundation.

"Till scarcely human feeling stirred his breast,
By Conscience's sting and dark Remorse opprest—
By Ghosts of buried sins, that crush and blast
The fairest hopes that Happiness would cast
'Ere they could form themselves in place —
Misfortune's gloomy child he'd been from birth,
For Death's unsparing hand had swept his hearth
Of relatives on whom he'd placed
A more than kindred love.   So sorrow traced
With iron hand, upon his brow her stamp
Of care; and Disappointment's chilling damp
Had blighted early peace.

JANUARY 1st, 1855. [10]

A PROSE POEM.

Another wave across the tide of Time
Has rolled! Another year into the Past
Has glided by!

The hand of Time but lightly touches those
Whose hearts are free from care.   Time's-footsteps
Lightly press the soil where flowery verdure
Springs, spontaneously, from teeming richness
Constantly refreshed by good and holy deeds.
And yet Time's shadows and the frosts of care
A withering blight must cast.   On some, the mark
So faint as scarcely to be seen : On some,
Its stamp so deep, that, from the moment
Of its printing, on each anxious face, the
World's keen eye can read, in furrow'd lines,
The record of a sorrowing Past — But rays
Of sunlight and of brilliant Promise gild
The Future they illume.

The memories of
The buried year within the hearts of all
Are shrined.   To some, with disappointments
And with sorrows clouded ; the cherished
Hopes, on whose foundations they had in
Fancy raised bright, air-build castles for
Future tenements of happiness ; have
Vanished, as before the raging storm wind's
Blast the morning mists are driven from the
Wooded mountain side.

Nations in their progress, too, are stamped
By Time's impress; and this Grand Old Year will,
Upon the page of History, long be marked
As one of great event.

While each proud steamer
Which old Ocean bears upon her heaving
Bosom to our shores, is looked with
Anxious expectations for, as bringing
Tidings of the stirring deeds that nations

In the East are now enacting.*   The test
Has come which forever marks supremacy
Of power 'mongst those whose rivalry so
Long has stood untried by arms.   To the " days
Of Old " strange contradiction this !   For then
The Cross against the Crescent was arrayed;
And now, the wandering West in silence sees
The Crescent's turbaned warriors stand
Beside the armies of two Christian kings,
In common cause arrayed against another
Christian Potentate.

                        While in this stern
Relentless war, with its " magnificently
Grand array ;" where hosts of Europe's mightiest
Nations are engaged — while daring deeds
Of arms are done; before which Feudal valor,
And the storied deeds " of Old " have faded —
While carnage strews the pleasant fields which
Ere-while Peace had blest — While countless hordes
Of ruthless men are scattering woe and

                *The Crimean War.

Desolation in their path — while weeping
Mothers' mourn their stalwart sons destroyed;
And drooping widows, helpless orphans wait
In vain for the return of him whose
Honest toil sustained them, or by whose
Smile their fireside was cheered — while all
The thousand ills, by war entailed, are
Devastating Europe's soil, our own fair
Land — The land of Freedom and of Promise!
The cherished heaven of the heart-sick and
Oppressed of other lands, is teeming with
Especial bounties from the hand of God.

With golden harvests has our land been blest;
Our peoples' industry its own reward.
No war! No Famine! No anxious dread of
Separation from our fireside joys, can
Fright us with phantom — peopled fears.
Peace, with all her blessings, we enjoy!
Plenty, as her sister, and her hand-maid,
Comes, and smiles of Future Promise
Shine upon our path.

Have we no thirst for
Fame ? Such thirst only as the good and free
Should have ? Not that of conquest for
Extended power, not of the blood-stained field,
Not of the ages and the nations long
Passed by, not of dominion and compulsive
Sway, where forced obedience to tyrant
Power may bend the common will to bow
And cringe before the mandate of a king,
To augment a Nation's glory by one man's fame.
Ours the grander claim ; that we ourselves
Can rule—And by a People's virtue raise
Our country's name to such high grade, and plant
Our country's honor on such firm base, that
After ages shall look back upon our
Page of fame, to admire the wisdom, which
Conceived the plan ; the Nation, whose firm will
Sustained it.

Close in the bands of brotherhood are joined
The States which form our Great Republic,
To their number each year adds.   Already
Do the waves of two great oceans wash

Our shores.   Already has our enterprise,
In far less time than infant colonies
By other nations are established,
Opened mines of countless golden wealth
Upon the Western Ocean's shores ; And
Already has a proud and splendid city
Sprung, Pallas like, into being at full growth.
New territory is each day being peopled
And new States are constantly laid out
Where but a few years since, the "foot of white man
Never trod."   Even now, by its roads of iron,
Is our Eastern sea-board country girded ;
And the path of progress is so far advanced
That iron roads, 'ere many years upon
The tide of Time have rolled, shall join the broad
Atlantic and Pacific Coasts.

Each passing year its tribute yields to our
Prosperity.   The "Starry Flag" the breeze
Of every sea shakes out.   Commerce,
With bounteous hand, is adding larger riches
To our stores.   Wealth multiplies ; and the

Beons that she confers, of cultivation
And refinement, are growing in inceased
Proportion.   Education is a gift
To all.   The children of the poor and rich,
Alike, enjoy the boon : and our youth
Have even in their view the goal they may attain,
By industry and truth, of competence,
Of ease, perhaps of fame and of high station.

Blest with such bounties from the hand of God —
Of peace, prosperity, a teeming soil,
Religion, wealth, brave hearts and such liberty
Of word and deed as Freeman prize, where
Liberty accords with Law, where can
Another land be found so favored and
So fair ? — The mystic stories of the East
Have scarcely pictured dreams in colors
Bright as our realities.

And now, as the old year into the Past
Has glided by, and left such record on
The page of Time ; and as each New Year is
Ushered in with promise such as this one

Gilds, in brilliant prestige, for our Nation's

Glory, collective weal should compensate

For such misfortunes and such sorrow

As some of us have borne.   And thankfulness

To God for boons we have, should fill our hearts

With pride of Country, and with praise of Him,

Rather than grief, despair, or dark repining

At seeming ills which may be shadowed

For our good.

NOTES.

Note I.—"*Old Virginia Land.*"

Written in Baltimore, in July 1862, to my wife then at the North.

Note II.—"*Maryland Battle Song.*

"Nor trust for peace to words." A compromise was made on Sunday, April 21, 1861, between the Municipal Authorities of Baltimore and the U. S. Government, by which it was agreed that the troops, then at Cockneysville on march to the Capitol should not pass through the City of Baltimore.

Note III.—"*Election Ode.*"

Written on the day previous to the Presidential Election in 1856, on a bet that I would, within twenty minutes, write an "Election Ode," which, without regard to party would be published the next morning, in any political paper in New York City to which it might be offered.

The bet was won and the Ode appeared in the *New York Express.*

Note IV.—"*In Memoriam.*"

The author while spending an evening with a neighbor, a German, was requested by him to versify his crudely expressed ideas, in memory of a friend and countryman, who had died of cholera, and from whose funeral he had but then returned.

The deceased was highly respected and esteemed for many noble traits of character — was a merchant of large wealth, and a mason in high standing.

Note V.—" *The Shipwreck.*"

The clipper ship Fanny S. Purley sailed from New York for San Francisco in 1860. Never heard from.

Note VI.—"*Clouds.*"

In answer to the following lines by an unknown poet.

"A cloud upon the sky—
Flowers close their cups, the butterfly his wing,
The restless birds all cease at once to sing,
    The shivering leaves foretell a storm is nigh ;
Let the gray evening darken into night,
To-morrow's sun will only shine more bright.
    Such cloud as these pass by."

"A cloud upon the heart—
What pleased of late has lost its charm to-day ;
    The trust undoubting seems misplaced and bold ;
    The kindly words sound distant, stiff and cold ;
The form remains, the life has passed away ;
    Each shrouded spirit acts its former part.
Still smile meets smile, but heart is far from heart.
    Will this dark cloud depart ?

"What wrought the clouds we mourn ?
Was it the truth, outspoken, love should hide ?
    Was it some want of reverence in playful mood,
    Some thought confided, and not understood,
Some promise broken, or some shock of pride ?
    Enough they 've risen—grief and tears were vain,
After this darkness and these bursts of rain.
    Such clouds return, or shall remain."

Note VII.—" *An Indian Funeral in Mexico.*"

On an evening in the Spring of 1850, when a band of California emigrants had encamped on the outskirts of a village, between Tampico and San Luis Potosi, and, after a long day's march, were sleeping by their watch fires, they were aroused by sounds of a large body of men marching towards them, singing a strange monotonous dirge, accompanied by shrieks and shouts in chorus.

After the procession had passed their guide informed them that it was a Mexican Indian Funeral ; and that the shouts and songs were incantations to keep off the demons, who the Indians, in their traditional superstitions, believed would attempt to take possession of the body and soul of the dead.

Note VIII.—" *Hope On.*"

Written for my wife, when anxious for her father's safety from shipwreck.

He was drowned on January 23, 1867 ; but the fact was not known until a month later.

Note IX—" *Fragment.*"

From memory, from " The Sceptic," a poem written many years ago—MSS. lost.

Note X—" *January* 1, 1855."

Written for a New York weekly. Mark the contrast of this picture to that of the years of the late civil war 1861 to 1865.